Anonymous

The Right Honourable Annuitant Vindicated

With a word or two in favour of the other great man, in case of his

resignation. In a letter to a friend in the country

Anonymous

The Right Honourable Annuitant Vindicated
*With a word or two in favour of the other great man, in case of his resignation. In a
letter to a friend in the country*

ISBN/EAN: 9783337194833

Printed in Europe, USA, Canada, Australia, Japan

Cover: Foto ©Andreas Hilbeck / pixelio.de

More available books at **www.hansebooks.com**

THE

RIGHT HONOURABLE

ANNUITANT

VINDICATED.

WITH

A Word or two in Favour of the *other*
GREAT MAN, in Cafe of his
RESIGNATION.

In a LETTER to

A FRIEND in the COUNTRY.

LONDON:

Printed for J. MORGAN, in *Pater-noſter Row.*
MDCCLXI.

(Price One Shilling.)

THE

RIGHT HONOURABLE

ANNUITANT

VINDICATED.

DEAR SIR,

HErewith I fend you the *London Ga-zette*, by which you will fee that the important paragraphs of news, to which you would not give any credit in the common papers, are confirmed by the higheft authority. I am always forry to differ from you in opinion; but cannot help thinking that on this occafion you

have

have exerted lefs than your ufual candour.
The *Great Commoner* has, in my mind,
thrown up his employments with the
fame honour and the fame fpirit of difin-
tereftednefs that he took them up. He
has retired with only a new dignity an-
nexed to his family, and an ANNUITY,
fo fmall, fo very inconfiderable and inade-
quate to the purpofes of luxury and corruption, that he has been obliged to fet
his Coach Horfes to fale by publick Ad-
vertifement. There is nothing fo moving,
faith *Seneca*, as a great man in diftrefs.
What can be more melancholy than a ftatef-
man on the *pavèe* ?—Yet has our bright
Sun of Patriotifm fet with no lefs glory
than he rofe. He has received the Royal
Thanks—he was *very near* receiving the
City Thanks—and has gone out of power
with

with the fame *unembarraffed Countenance*
that he came in.

There are, I think, three modes of mi-
nifterial Refignation. The firft is, when a
Great Patriot conceives a difguft at the bafe-
nefs of any meafures propofed by his com-
panions in the Adminiftration, and from a
noble indignation quits their fellowfhip,
left his countrymen fhould account him
a fharer in their guilt.—This feems to be
the moft fimple and natural method, but
is neverthelefs much the moft uncom-
mon. The fecond is, when a Minifter,
in the ftile of the news-papers, *refigns,*
but is, in good truth, fairly *turned out.*—
This method has been practifed within
all our memories. The third is, when a
Minifter, for the convenience of the Go-

B 2 vernment,

vernment, refigns by private compact and
agreement, and receives a certain *douceur*
for his compliance.—This, thanks to the
complaifance and humanity of the times,
is the moft modern mode : and to this the
pliant and amiable temper of our GREAT
COMMONER has chofen to fubmit.

But this, it feems, it is, which, being
barely fuggefted in a news-paper, was capable of alarming you fo fenfibly, and of
touching you to the quick with indignation
and furprife.—What mere Weathercocks
are you Country Gentlemen !—Once you
looked upon this fhining Meteor in politicks
with diflike.   Afterwards, on his efforts to
make his way into the cabinet, and take
the reins of power into his hands, you
feconded his attempts, threw your whole
weight

weight into his fcale, and prompted every
corporation in *England* to honour him with
their freedom in gold-boxes. But now you
revert to your firft principles, and begin
to revive your antient fentiments of difap-
probation.—And why ? or wherefore ?—
In order to give your arguments, fuch as
they are, fair play, fuffer me to ftate all that
you have urged, or can urge, in cenfure of
the conduct of our GREAT COMMONER.

Firft then, you may fay, that it is very
unlike a Patriot to retire from the Adminiftration of public affairs, at a time when
the nation appears to be moft in want of his
affiftance.—That to fay he refigned his
employments becaufe he found it impoffi-
ble to render to his country fuch fervices
as he intended, is a weak plea ; fince it is
evident

evident, that had he refigned them in a
proper manner, the voice of the people
would have obliged him to refume them,
and the meafures he propofed, if at all
plaufible, would certainly have been per-
fued.

Secondly, That to retire with a PENSION,
was to retire with ignominy and difgrace,
in direct contradiction to the principles,
which he has all along fo openly avowed
and profeffed.

To give thefe arguments the more force,
let us fuppofe, That on the propofal of fuch
terms to our GREAT COMMONER, as he
appears to have accepted, that he, with the
voice and gefture of *Demofthenes*, had re-
plied fomewhat in the following manner.

4 " No·

" No.—Far be it from me ever to aſſent
' to terms, ſo derogatory to my honour,
" ſo unworthy of a Lover of his Country!
" Terms, at whoſe abject meanneſs I am
" ſhocked and diſguſted, and whoſe CRI-
" MINALITY I conſider with horrour:—
" Terms, *which would hang, like a* MILL-
" STONE, *about the neck of the Miniſter*,
" who ſhould diſgrace himſelf by his ac-
" ceptance of them, and plunge him into
" the loweſt gulph of popular contempt.—
" What part of my conduct could ever
" inſpire my moſt bitter enemy with the
" lighteſt hope that I could be *bought off*
" from my duty, or that my name ſhould
" ever be enrolled in the catalogue of PEN-
" SIONERS? Have I not always endea-
" voured to diſtinguiſh myſelf by my con-
" tempt of money?—Did I not publickly
" re-

" refign to better ufes the perquifites of
" lucrative employments !—And was not
" the firft confiderable acquifition to my
" fortune evidently made by the integrity
" of my conduct, and the fteadinefs of my
" oppofition, to the meafures of corrup-
" tion and venality ?—Whence, I befeech
" you, is the annual Sum, to which this
" Pension amounts, to iffue ?—It muft
" neceffarily be taken either from the pub-
" lic money or the Civil Lift.--And fhall I
" lie like a burden or heavy impoft on the
" People; or fuffer myfelf or my family
" to become a Rent-Charge on the King?—
" No ! it would ill become me, after fuch
" a condefcenfion, to take my feat again in
" *that houfe*, where I have fo often decla-
" red, That it would be better for that
" houfe,

" houfe *, *if new parliaments were more*
" *frequent, and few Placemen, and No* PEN-
" SIONERS *admitted.*—Or with what grace
" can I permit my Practice to contradict
" my Theory, and prevail on myfelf to
" contribute towards running the Civil Lift
" into debt? when I have alfo laid it down
" as a maxim, that, ‡ *It is inconfiftent with*
" *the honour of this nation to have our King*
" *ftand indebted to his fervants or tradefmen,*
" *who may be ruined by a delay of payment :*
" *The Parliament has provided fufficiently*
" *for preventing this difhonour's being brought*
" *upon the nation ; and if the Provifion we*
" *have made fhould be* MISAPPLIED *or* LA-
" VISHED, *we muft fupply the deficiency ; we*
" *ought to do it, whether the king makes*

* *Chandler's* Debates, vol. xiii. p. 172.
‡ Ibid. p. 214.

C
any

" *any application for that purpose, or no.—*
" After such a declaration I should blush to
" divert the stream of his M——y's munifi-
" cence into so mean a channel, or to draw
" my life and being from that source. I,
" that stood against corruption in my youth,
" will not set my integrity to bargain and
" sale in my old age; for,* *much, very much,*
" *is he to be abhorred, who, as he has ad-*
" *vanced in age, has receded from Virtue,*
" *and becomes more wicked with less Tempta-*
" *tion; who prostitutes himself for money*
" *which he cannot enjoy, and spends the re-*
" *mains of his life in the ruin of his country.*
" Rather, therefore, let me cherish ‡ *that*
" *Zeal for the service of my country, which*
" *neither* HOPE *nor* FEAR *shall influence me*
" *to suppress. I will not sit* UNCONCERNED
" *while my Liberty is invaded, nor look in si-*

" *lence*

* *Chandler's* Debates, vol. xii. p. 282.
‡ Ibid. p. 283.

" *lence upon* PUBLIC ROBBERY. *I will*
" *exert my endeavours, at whatever hazard,*
" *to repel the Aggreſſor, and drag the Thief*
" *to Juſtice, whoever may protect them in their*
" *villainy, and whoever may partake of their*
" *plunder.*"

In theſe rhetorical flouriſhes I think is
contained all that can be advanced, with the
leaſt juſtice or propriety, in cenſure of the
conduct of our illuſtrious commoner; nor
can it be denied but that I have given them
their full force, ſince I have introduced
many of his own words, and ſome of thoſe
notable ſentiments which he himſelf once
vollied out; with all the dreadful artillery
of eloquence, againſt the GREAT MAN of
that day. But then it muſt be remembered,
that we have not yet heard him on the

other

other fide of the queftion. We have not
yet feen him levelling the thunder of his
oratory againft the enemies of placemen
and Penfioners. It is uncandid and ungenerous to condemn him, before you have
heard what he has to fay in his defence.
Audi alteram partem! If, in confirmity to
your fuggeftions, I have forced thefe words
into his mouth again, I warrant you, he is
capable of eating them, ay, and of digeft-
ing them into the bargain. It is not the
firft time, that he has fpoke in favour of
thofe very meafures, which he once reviled; and having firft taught us to hold
them in abomination, afterwards reconci-
led us to his purfuit of them. If, after
the warmeft declarations againft *continental
connections*—if after the ftrongeft oppofition
to remitting either men or money to *Ger-*

many

many, and a downright refufal to confent to. give the D--ke of *C*——*d* any affiftance there, though in the moft deplorable cir-cumftances—If, I fay, after all this, he could himfelf embrace *continental connec-tions*, if he could fend over men by ten thoufands, and money by hundred thou-fands, and nobody be in the leaft offended or furprized——why may not he alfo, who has railed fo long at PENSIONS and PENSION-ERS, at laft take a PENSION *himfelf*, and prove to the fatisfaction of the whole world, that it is not the *thing done*, but the *how*, and the *why*, and the *when*, and by *whom* it is *done*, that conftitutes the CRIMINALI-TY and offence!—May he not tell us, that three thoufand pounds *per* Year is a poor reward for all his great and important fer-vices? And may he not confider it as a kind

of

of petty tribute from his rich conquefts in the *Eaft* and *Weft Indies*, on the Coaft of *France*, and on the *Ocean?* May he not plead his right to an *Otium cum dignitate?* May he not convince us of our miftake in imagining that VIRTUE *is its own reward?* and may he not tell us, that if we fuppofe the ftreets of *London* to be paved with filver and gold, we are as much to blame, as he is now fenfible he was himfelf, when he pronounced the ftreets of *Oxford* to be *paved with Difaffection* and *Jacobitifm?*

Thefe things, with many others of equal weight, would undoubtedly fuggeft themfelves to our GREAT MAN, even in an *extempore* reply to the charge brought againft him, and even if it was taken on your own reprefentation. But the accu-
fation

fation is not fairly laid. He is neither unjuft nor inconfiftent. He has inveighed againft PENSIONERS, it is true; and he may ftill continue to do fo, for he has *no* PENSION.—No! what then?—Why, Sir, he has *an* ANNUITY—An ANNUITY—Not a bit of a PENSION, I affure you—for, as *Foigard* wifely diftinguiſhes, " if you take " it *beforehand* it is a BRIBE, but if you " take it *afterwards, it is only a* GRATI" FICATION."—This is no *Bribe*, but a *Reward*, as witnefs *Quebec, Louifburg, Senegal, Goree, Guadalupe, Bellifle, &c. &c. &c. &c. &c. &c. &c.*—and is indeed no more than, when an old faithful fervant gives warning that he will *leave his place*, juft kindly difmiffing him with a month's wages. He has taken an ANNUITY then it is true, but no PENSION—only an AN-

NUITY

NUITY for his own life, his Lady's life, and the life of his eldeſt Son—that is, an Annuity *for three lives,* for which I heard a Broker at *Jonathan's* ſay, that he would give Fifty Thouſand Pounds, if it ever came into the Alley. An Annuity may alſo have ſome other properties different from a Pension. Pensions are ſubject to a Tax—an Annuity may perhaps be exempt from this inconvenience, and be eſtabliſhed to be paid out of the privy purſe *clear of all deductions:* and in that caſe, if it ſhould ever go to market, my friend at *Jonathan's* muſt allow that the Purchaſe-money would be ſtill more conſiderable.—It muſt be allowed therefore that a Pension and an Annuity are no more the ſame thing than an Egg and a Chicken—a *Penſion* is but an *Annuity* in embrio,

embrio, but an *Annuity* is a *Penfion* brought
to perfection and maturity.—At the firft ex-
hibition of a *ridotto* in this country, the
people were confounded at the novelty of
the term, and did not know what it meant:
upon which a wag ftuck a paper to the back
of one of the company, fignifying, in
large letters, *this is the* RIDOTTO. In like
manner I would humbly propofe, in order to diftinguifh this GREAT MAN from
the mean *Band of Penfioners*, that a label
be fixed to his back, with an infcription
wrought in gold letters, like the G. R. on
the cloaths of the beef-eaters, fignifying
in magnificent capitals, THIS IS THE
ANNUITANT.

I am forry, my dear fir, that you force
me to ftop here to anfwer the contraft

you

you have drawn between this *Great Man* and the other gentleman, who was honoured at the fame time with himfelf, with the gold boxes.—HE, you fay, retired without any *Penfion*, nay even without an *Annuity*; and refufed all reward or confideration for his fervices, except a title for his Lady, to which fhe had a kind o_f *hereditary* claim. Why, Sir—if this be true—I — I — I — that is——to be fure ——you know, Sir—there is fome kind of——In fhort I cannot difpute this point with you. Yet, notwithftanding your partiality to the gentleman you have inftanced, you muft allow that his political reputation has always been infinitely inferior to that of our *Great Man*. He has been no man of *words*, but of *deeds* only. His patriotifm never made *that noife* in the world

world which was occafioned by that of his colleague; and therefore could not fo well afford fuch a drawback from his fame. On the whole, I may venture to allow your friend to be in this inftance the fuperior character, and yet efteem the Great Commoner, *in the main,* as the moft eminent and illuftrious.—As to the dignity, in that affair he has behaved with as much modefty as his friend—nay, with ftill more—for the title by which he has chofen to diftinguifh his lady—*Lady Chat'em*——feems as if taken in jeft——It founds as ridiculous as king of *Brentford,* and feems merely calculated for one of the mock dignitaries in the *Dramatis Perfonæ* of a Comedy.

Prudence is univerfally allowed to be a great virtue—one of the cardinal vir-

tues

tues—and yet, by I know not what fatality, it often encounters contempt, and is received with much lefs admiration than the three other cardinal virtues of *Juftice*, *Temperance*, and *Fortitude:* though after all, Juftice could in real life never make any thing more than a judge; Temperance is a mere valetudinarian; and Fortitude a captain in the *militia* at beft; while Prudence might make a general, a ftatef-man, a monarch, or any illuftrious cha-racter under the fun. Prudence is the very life and foul of a GREAT MAN; and in the refignation of our illuftrious Com-moner, no virtue was more confpicuous than his Prudence. He *prudently* forefaw that there would be much trouble and dif-ficulty in fettling a peace to the liking of all ranks of people; wherefore he very

prudently

prudently quitted his employments; and afterwards very *prudently* alſo accepted a handſome proviſion for himſelf and his family.

Finding my brain big with matter on this part of the vindication of our GREAT MAN's character, and teeming with argument (inſomuch that I am only con-fuſed by the multiplicity of my materials, and at a loſs in what manner to arrange what I have to ſay) juſt at this time an ineſtimable original, moſt curious both as to its ſtile and matter, has offered itſelf, which not only corroborates all that has or can be advanced, but ſerves alſo to diſpoſe my ſentiments into method and order. The Country Journal of your own County has, I dare ſay, copied it

from

from our *London* papers, where I found
it; but as I fhall naturally make many
references and allufions to it, it may be
more convenient to have it all immediately before you. I have therefore tran-
fcribed it in this place.

A Letter from a Right Hon. Perfon to his
Friend in the City.

DEAR SIR,

'FINDING, to my great Surprife,
'   that the Caufe and Manner of my
' refigning the Seals, is grofsly mifrepre-
' fented in the City, as well as that the
' moft gracious and *fpontaneous* Marks of
' his Majefty's Approbation of my Ser-
' vices, which Marks followed my Re-
' fignation, have been infamoufly traduced

' as

‘ as a Bargain for my forſaking the Pub-
‘ lick, I am under a Neceſſity of declar-
‘ ing the Truth of both theſe Facts, in a
‘ Manner which I am ſure no Gentle-
‘ man will contradict: A Difference of
‘ Opinion with regard to Meaſures to be
‘ taken againſt *Spain*, of the higheſt Im-
‘ portance to the Honour of the Crown,
‘ and to the moſt eſſential national In-
‘ tereſts, (and this founded on what *Spain*
‘ had already done, not on what that
‘ Court may farther intend to do) was
‘ the Cauſe of my reſigning the Seals.
‘ Lord TEMPLE and I ſubmitted, in
‘ Writing, and ſigned by us, our moſt
‘ humble Sentiments to his Majeſty, which
‘ being over-ruled by the united Opinion
‘ of all the reſt of the King’s Servants, I
‘ reſigned the Seals on Monday the 5th of
‘ this

' this Month, in Order not to remain re-
' fponfible for Meafures, which I was no
' longer allowed to guide. Moft graci-
' ous publick Marks of his Majefty's Ap-
' probation of my Services followed my
' Refignation : They are unmerited and
' unfolicited, and I fhall ever be proud to
' have received them from the beft of
' Sovereigns.

' I will now only add, my dear Sir,
' that I have explained thefe Matters only
' for the Honour of Truth, not in any
' View to court return of Confidence from
' any Man, who with a Credulity, as
' weak as it is injurious, has thought fit
' haftily to withdraw his good Opinion,
' from one who has ferved his Country
' with Fidelity and Succefs; and who

' juftly

' juftly reveres the upright and candid
' Judgment of it ; little folicitous about the
' cenfures of the Capricious and the Un-
' generous : Accept my fincereft Acknow-
' ledgments for all your kind Friendfhip,
' and believe me ever with Truth and
' Efteem,

> ' My Dear Sir,

>> ' Your faithful Friend, &c.'

And now, my dear Sir, let me afk you,
if every word of this moft valuable letter does not afford a ftrong confirmation
of our Great Man's Prudence. It affords
alfo an equal proof of his candour and
veracity, *which I am fure no Gentleman
will contradict :* for it *declares the Truth of
both thefe Facts* to be, juft what we all

E   con-

conceived it to be before this epiftle to his friend in the City was made publick. Perhaps, however, you rough boifterous country gentlemen might mifapprehend this matter. You might poffibly imagine, that he went bluntly to his Mafter, and faid, " Sir, if you will give me an *An-* " *nuity* of three thoufand *per* year, I will " refign,"—and fo the Bargain was ftruck. —But how little agreeable would fuch a conduct be to his *Prudence?* Mark, how different the cafe really was. *Moft gra-cious publick marks of approbation of my fervice* FOLLOWED *my refignation. Fol-lowed*—Sir, do you obferve ?—and he knew that they *would follow* if he chofe it—To be fure, he did; and there, Sir, there was the *Prudence. They* (that is the *Marks*) *are unmerited and unfolicited——*

here

here again, Sir, his Prudence and Fore-
fight are remarkable—He very *prudently*
left *unfolicited* that which he knew would
follow, and which he knew that he would
not refufe. Modeftly, therefore, to fay
they are UNMERITED, means no more
than the *Nolo Epifcopari* of a Bifhop E-
lect, who is neverthelefs equally fure of
his Epifcopacy.—Your inflexible *Britifh*
Spirit, ftubborn as our Oak itfelf, may
perhaps feel itfelf offended at fome of
the following expreffions. *Lord* T. *and I*
fubmitted in Writing, and figned by us,
our moft humble fentiments to his Majefty,
which being over-ruled by the united Opinion
of all the reft of the King's Servants, I
refigned the Seals on Monday the 5th of this
Month, in order not to remain refponfible

for

*for Meafures, which I was no longer al-
lowed to* Guide.——This, perhaps, you
will fay, is acting and talking like his
Mafter's Mafter, inftead of his humble
Servant, a kind of Lord Paramount over
both K—g and M——y.——Not at all.
—Every fervant of his M——y, as well
as of any other perfon in *England,* is
at liberty to leave his *Place* when he
pleafes; and to leave it juft when there is
the moft need of his affiftance, only tends
to heighten his confequence, and to fhew
that he is *one who has ferved his country
with* Fidelity *and* Success.—Did not
feveral of the Greateft Men in the kingdom defert his late M——y, and throw
up their employments, juft when he was
moft in need of their fervices? and were
not they all reinftated in their places?

4   May

May not therefore the GREAT MAN of our times too refign in the very Crifis of our affairs? and though he refufes to do any more for us, need he alfo refufe a reward for what he has done?—Well but then—*Meafures, which I was no longer allowed to* GUIDE.—Thefe, my friend, thefe, I fee, are the words which you cannot digeft, and which you think unbecoming the mouth of a private fubject, nay almoft even of a K—g in this country.——But let not your high ftomach be offended at them. Our GREAT MAN has always habituated himfelf to a Grandeur of expreffion, as well as an elevation of fentiment. It would not be aftonifhing therefore, if he fhould now and then appear fomewhat abfolute; but in the prefent inftance, he is a pattern of humility.

humility.—Take the whole fentence together, you will find that it is entirely
metaphorical, and will admit of the
mildeft interpretation. *Lord* T. *and I fubmitted in Writing, and figned by us, our moft
humble Sentiments to his Majefty, which being over-ruled by the united opinion* of all
the reft of the King's Servants, *I refigned
the Seals on Monday the 5th of this Month,
in order not to remain refponfible for meafures, which I was no longer allowed to* GUIDE.
Here you fee he confiders the council as fo
many fervants in a family. One perhaps as
the *Maitre d'hotel*, another as the Butler, a
third as my lord's *own man*, and the reft
as fo many footmen, helpers, *&c.* To himfelf he feems to have affigned the province
of the *Coachman*; and, in this fituation,
he has a right to remonftrate againft their

pro-

proceedings: for to propofe *meafures, which he is no longer allowed to* GUIDE, while he is yet upon the box, is abfolutely taking the whip and reins out of his hands. Suppofe you were in your Coach and Six on a long journey in the middle of winter, in deep roads and bad weather, and that on the coachman's preparing to fhew his fkill in driving to an inch by the edge of a precipice, *the reft of the fervants* were to bawl out to him to ftop, and you yourfelf fhould infift on his going another way : In thefe circumftances, Sir, only fuppofe that the *Coachman* was to defcend from his box, and coming to the coach door accoft you in thefe terms : " Sir, You have been *the* " *beft of mafters* to me, it is true, but if I " go any other way than my own, I'll be " d——d.—I never overturned you in my " life,

" life, and if you will *no longer allow me*
" *to* GUIDE, why then, by G—d, neither
" I, nor the *Poſtillion*, will drive you an
" inch further, and ſo you may get home
" as you can."—Now, Sir, in ſuch a caſe,
·though you might not chuſe to run the riſk
of the precipice, or much like being left
in the lurch if you declined it, yet, if he
had been a good coachman, I do not ſee
how you could juſtify refuſing him a character. Nay, perhaps, if he had ſerved
you well, and was a favourite in the family,
you would very probably give him and his
wife *ſome little matter* to ſet up with in buſineſs, if they choſe it, on quitting your
place.—This is directly the caſe of our
GREAT MAN—This is the very CAUSE
AND MANNER *of his reſigning the Seals*—
and yet this has been *groſsly miſrepreſented*

in

in the City, as well as the most gracious and spontaneous *marks of his Majesty's approbation of his services, which marks,* followed *his resignation, infamously traduced as a Bargain for his forsaking the Publick.* However, heaven be praised, he is and ever was *little solicitous about the censures of the Capricious and the Ungenerous,* and now he is retired from the Administration of public affairs, he is at leisure to pursue his private occupations. He may amuse himself with improving his little income in the alley, with buying out and selling in, and watching the various revolutions of the stocks: or he may lay it out in fashionable improvements of his house and gardens at *H—y—s:* or, if amidst the wonderful versatility of his Genius, he has any turn for Trade, he may, if he pleases, convert his

F   *An-*

Annuity into one large capital, and then, being free of the *Grocer's company*, you know he may go into partnerſhip with his friend the preſent L——d M--y--r, who is the moſt eminent in that buſineſs. In ſuch a caſe, at how many thouſand pounds might the very *good will* of the ſhop be rated at! Would not all ranks and degrees of people be his cuſtomers! Would not every Alderman's Cuſtard contain his Sugar and Nutmeg! Would not the *Sunday's* plum-pudding of every patriot mechanick be filled with his dried currants and raiſins? and would not every publick-ſpirited waſher-woman in town purchaſe her halfquartern of *Bohea* at that ſhop?

Having travelled thus far in vindication of the Right Honourable ANNUITANT, it
gives

gives me unfpeakable pleafure to find my fentiments of his Letter fall in fo exactly with thofe of the Gentleman in the City, to whom it was addreffed. The anfwer, which he returned, confiders the matter exactly in the fame light that I have done, the defence that he makes is exactly of the fame colour, and the reafons which he has urged in favour of his friend are equally ftrong and fatisfactory. But take it, as you have had the other, at full length.

LETTER TO A RIGHT HONOUR-ABLE PERSON.

DEAR SIR,

'THE City of *London*, as long as they have any Memory, cannot forget,

F 2 that

‘ that you accepted the Seals when this
‘ Nation was in the moſt deplorable Cir-
‘ cumſtances to which any Country can
‘ be reduced: That our Armies were
‘ beaten, our Navy inactive, our Trade
‘ expoſed to the Enemy, our Credit, as if
‘ we expected to become Bankrupts, ſunk
‘ to the loweſt Pitch, that there was no-
‘ thing to be found but Deſpondency at
‘ Home, and Contempt Abroad. The
‘ City muſt alſo for ever remember,
‘ that when you reſigned the Seals, our
‘ Armies and Navies were victorious, our
‘ Trade ſecure, and flouriſhing more than
‘ in a Peace, our Public Credit reſtored,
‘ and People readier to lend than Mini-
‘ ſters to borrow: That there was nothing
‘ but Exultation at Home, Confuſion and
‘ Deſpair among our Enemies, Amaze-
‘ ment

‘ ment and Veneration among all Neutral
‘ Nations: That the *French* were reduced
‘ fo low as to fue for a Peace, which we,
‘ from Humanity, were willing to grant;
‘ though their Haughtinefs was too great,
‘ and our Succeffes too many, for any
‘ Terms to be agreed on. Remembering
‘ this, the City cannot but lament that you
‘ have quitted the Helm. But if Knaves
‘ have taught Fools to call your Refigna-
‘ tion, (when you can no longer procure
‘ the fame Succefs, being prevented from
‘ purfuing the fame Meafures) a Defertion
‘ of the Publick, and to look upon you,
‘ for accepting a Reward, which can fcarce
‘ bear that Name, in the Light of a Pen-
‘ fioner; the City of *London* hope, they
‘ fhall not be ranked by you among the
‘ one or the other. They are truly fenfible,

' ble, that, though you ceafe to guide the
' Helm, you have not deferted the Veffel;
' and that, Penfioner as you are, your In-
' clination to promote the publick Good,
' is ftill only to be equalled by your Abi-
' lity: That you fincerely wifh Succefs to
' the new Pilot, and will be ready, not
' only to warn him and the Crew of Rocks
' and Quickfands, but to affift in bringing
' the Ship through the Storm into a fafe
' Harbour.

" Thefe, Sir, I am perfuaded, are the
" real Sentiments of the City of *London*; I
" am fure you believe them to be fuch of,

DEAR SIR,

Your, &c.

With

With what pathetick energy hath this *anfwering* Citizen recapitulated the great actions of his friend !—The good he has done us by coming into power, the evil that may enfue from his going out, and that he has, it feems, the whole city in a ftring, are circumftances, which, (to ufe the Anfwerer's words) *as long as we have any memory, we cannot forget.* You may perceive alfo in this anfwer fomething of the fame complexion with my illuftration of the Office of Minifter, by the character of a *Coachman;* only that the judicious *Anfwerer* has with the utmoft propriety, in this our maritime nation, tranfported the allufion from land to fea. Obferve his words ! *The* C I T Y *cannot but lament that you have quitted the* H E L M. *But they are truly fenfible, that,*

though

though you ceafe to GUIDE THE HELM,
you have not deferted the veffel: and that,
PENSIONER AS YOU ARE, *your inclina-*
tion to promote the publick good, is ftill only
to be equalled by your Ability: That you fin-
cerely wifh fuccefs to the new PILOT, *and*
will be ready, not only to warn HIM *and*
the CREW *of* ROCKS *and* QUICKSANDS,
but to affift in bringing the SHIP *through*
the STORM *into a fafe* HARBOUR.—With
how much grandeur has the *Anfwerer*,
even in the familiarity of the epiftolary
ftile, maintained this noble allufion! The
allegorical genius of *Bunyan* himfelf could
not have purfued it with more ftrict propriety and fuccefs; or rather, to raife my
comparifon, the *Anfwerer* has rivaled
even *Horace* in that exalted Ode, wherein
he likens the Commonwealth to a *Ship:*

nay,

nay, he has even furpaffed the *Roman*
Poet, for by adding the *particular Cuftoms*
of our Age and Country to the *general*
turn of the Allufion, which both writers
poffefs in common with each other, he
has moft wonderfully ftrengthened and
enforced it, and carried it much further
than the *Latin* Lyrick could poffibly do.
It is well known that the noble fpirit of
charity and munificence, fo peculiar to
this country, gave rife to the noble infti-
tutions of *Chelfea* and *Greenwich* Colleges,
for the fupport of decayed Veterans in
our fervice both by land and fea ; and it
is alfo further known that the old or difabled foldiers and feamen maintained by
thefe charities are called PENSIONERS.
To this it is that we owe, in the midft of
fuch a cloud of naval terms, the intro-
duction

duction of thofe remarkable words, PEN-
SIONER AS YOU ARE. The elegant Anfwerer, while he confiders the State as a
Ship; the holding the feals as *guiding the
helm*; the Minifter as the *Pilot*; the people,
or perhaps only the Members of the H——
of C———ns, as the *Crew*; bad Meafures
as *Rocks* and *Quickfands*; War as a *Storm*;
and Peace as the *Harbour*;——at the
fame time heightens the fimilitude by
looking on the Right Honourable Annuitant as a *Greenwich*-College PENSION-
ER: by which ingenious allufion to our
own imes and manners, he not only
far tranfcends the Simplicity of *Horace*,
but alfo furnifhes us with an admirable
idea of *Penfioners* in general. In both
thefe Colleges, there are what they call
In-PENSIONERS, and *Out*-PENSIONERS——
fome,

fome, who conftitute, as it were, the family of the Hofpital, and others who
may be faid to be kept on Board-Wages.
—And perhaps the only, or at leaft the
beft, Reafon, why the whole Band of
Court-PENSIONERS are not embodied and
fupported together in a college of this
nature, is, that the number of *In*-PEN-
SIONERS is fo very fmall in comparifon to
that of the *Out*-PENSIONERS. The Right
Honourable ANNUITANT, having refigned the Seals, is become, like many more
of his Cotemporaries and Predeceffors, an
Out-PENSIONER: but yet, PENSIONER AS
HE IS, we are told, that he is not, like
the reft of the *College*, a difabled mariner
—a decayed veteran that has loft either
his ftrength or abilities in the fervice—but
one that has both inclination and ability

for

for the public fervice ftill remaining—one that is ready to *warn*, as well as to *affift.* ——In this new light, wherein the *Anfwerer* has exhibited his friend, he may be confidered as a broken officer, who is ftill retained on half-pay, and remains ready to be called out on any future occafions of fervice—at leaft he may be faid to have the benefit of the *College*, while he is ftill on board the veffel; or, what is ftill more defirable, he is at liberty to *lie by* and receive his pay, or help to work the Ship, juft as he pleafes. He may fwing at eafe in his hammock, in the midft of the ftorm, and content himfelf, like the *Irifhman*, with faying, *that he is only a Paffenger*; or he may haul a cable, reef a fail, make his voice and his whiftle as rough and as loud as the Boatfwain's,

3   and

and be as bufy aftern or abaft, below or aloft, as any man in the veffel.——In a word—to fet the fimile adrift, and fpeak in plain terms, our GREAT MAN has now moft *prudently* thrown himfelf into a fituation, in which he may, even with more confiftency than heretofore, embrace any meafures, however oppofite or contradictory. He is ready, as the Anfwerer tells us, either to *warn or to affift :* that is, he is ready, juft as occafion fhall ferve, either to acquiefce peaceably in the meafures of the Adminiftration, as other PENSIONERS have done; or elfe to exhibit himfelf to the world in the very new and fingular character of a PENSIONER IN OPPOSITION— a PATRIOT-PENSIONER, or in its proper and peculiar phrafe, a *Right Honourable* ANNUITANT.

To

To you perhaps, my dear Sir, it may appear ſtrange and unaccountable, that he ſhould be able to reconcile to each other two ſuch contradictory characters; and that while he eats the bread of the court, he ſhould oppoſe the meaſures of the Admini-ſtration. But this, Sir, is the diſtinguiſh-ing excellence of his temper and conduct. Your ſtubborn patriotiſm, like the needle ſtedfaſt to the pole, points always one way; but the new mode of patriotiſm, like the weathercock changing with every wind, knows how to veer and turn, and is ready to adapt itſelf to times and their ſeaſons, things and their circumſtances—*In* or *out*— *for* or *againſt*—juſt as their convenience ſuits, or occaſion requires.—*Demoſthenes*, the great Orator of *Greece*, forfeited the reputation of integrity, which he had al-

ways

ways maintained till that period, by receiv_
ing a bribe from *Harpalus*, in consequence
of which he appeared in the assembly,
muffled about the throat, and made signs,
that he was not able to deliver a Syllable.
It appears from hence, that it was not the
receiving the bribe, but the holding his
peace, by which *Demosthenes* injured his
fame. But our great Orator is ready to
convince the world, that no *Reward* shall
tie his tongue, or bind his hands; and
that it shall not be imputed to him, as it
was to *Demosthenes*, that he is affected
with a *Gold* or *Silver Quinsy*.—I have just
mentioned *Demosthenes*, because in the list
of patriots it is always usual to thunder out
a long muster-roll of *Greek* and *Roman*
Names: but I will venture to say that there
is no Patriot of all antiquity more eminent

and

and illuftrious, than our Great Commoner
has proved himfelf to be in his late Refignation.—If the elder *Brutus* is fo much to
be commended, becaufe he could prevail
on himfelf to give up the neareft and deareft
part of his family to publick juftice, how
much more applaufe is due to our modern
Brutus, who could manifeft his confidence
in the publick and love to his family at one
and the fame time, by throwing *them*, as
well as himfelf, on his country for fupport?
If the other old *Roman*, who, when he
left the affairs of the publick, retired to his
farm and turnips—-But it is vain and need-
lefs to recur to *Greece* and *Rome* for com-
parifons, or to draw parallels between the
Great Men of Antiquity and thofe of our
own times, when we can fo much more properly compare our cotemporary ftatefmen

to

to each other. Indeed, when I confider with how much *prudence* the Right Hon. Annuitant has withdrawn himfelf from bufinefs, juft when it was likely to become moft troublefome; what a fnug provifion he has acquired for himfelf in his retirement; and how calm and unconcerned he may fit amidft the general hurry and confufion;—I cannot compare him fo juftly to any other object, as to the *other* Great Man, who has fo long been the moft principal director of our affairs. That accomplifhed *M———r*, on a late publick occafion, found himfelf in a fituation exactly parallel to that of our Great Commoner at prefent. In the midft of the noife and buftle of the Coronation, he retired, unobferved by all, to the *Privy Chamber*, where fome ladies of the Court accidentally dif-

covered him *eafing himfelf* moft philofo-
phically of every troublefome appendage
to luxury and greatnefs, enjoying the com-
fort of his retreat, *ftraining* beyond the
reach of vulgar faculties, and furrounded
with every fymptom of felicity and *good luck*.

Having accidentally mentioned the *other*
Great Man, I cannot conclude this tedious
Letter, without adding a word or two in
his favour : and as it is the opinion of many
perfons, and, I fear, the invidious wifh
of many more, that he likewife will fhortly
find it expedient to *refign*, I think that the
Crown and the People are each bound in
honour and gratitude to make *him*, alfo a
handfome appointment, as well as the Right
Hon. Annuitant. It would be hard indeed,
as *Mat Prior* has it, *if one moufe eats while*
t'other

t'other ſtarves ; or that we ſhould take ſuch provident care of our *right-hand* Stateſman, and leave our helpleſs *left-handed* Miniſter in the lurch ; ſince he is at leaſt a *limb* of the *body politick*, though not of equal uſe with his *fellow*. He has been ſo groſsly reviled for the wretched peace, which he *hammered out* for us in 1748 ; that I doubt he will ſcarce try his hand to *tinker up* another. I beg leave therefore (as I own myſelf under obligations to him) to urge a few arguments in his behalf, to ſhew why he ought to be allowed at leaſt as good a *Penſion*, if an *Annuity* be thought too peculiar an indulgence, as any of thoſe eminent perſonages, who have lately been removed : and I much queſtion, notwithſtanding the great number of his own extraordinary largeſſes of this nature, whether he will

H 2 find

find many men, befides myfelf, thus grate-
ful to him, when he is out of Power. And
the firft general Reafon I will prefume to
give, is this:

That it would be a difgrace indeed upon the Government and the whole nation,
if *be alone* fhould go unrewarded for his
long, wonderful, and inexpreffible fervices. I believe I may venture to affert,
that fcarce any body of late has been difmif-
fed without *this publick mark of approbation
following their refignation.*--And why fhould
he?——Some, perhaps, who belong to
the honourable lift of Penfioners, have had
their names more carefully and *prudently*
concealed than others; but if the truth
was known, and a fair and honeft Regifter
of *Penfioners* was made out, and laid before
the

the Publick, I am perfuaded, we fhould find many great and worthy names, that have long lain dormant, and fuch as few, except the honourable fraternity themfelves, ever could fufpect.

Another ftrong argument in his favour is, that he has been as long in a *lucrative employment*, if not longer, than moft of his predeceffors or cotemporaries, and confequently deferves as large, if not a larger *Penfion*, than any of them.—This is but ftrict juftice according to the invariable *golden* rule of modern politicks.

A further reafon for putting this act of gratitude fpeedily in execution, is, that, fuch of late has been the profufion of grants of this nature, that there is fome doubt whether

there

there will otherwife be treafure fufficient to
anfwer fo large a demand left in the Ex-
ch—r. It may be neceffary perhaps, on this
occafion, to call in aid *anotherkingdom*, which
is tolerably well loaded already, and will
fcarce be able to receive many more of thefe
worthy gentlemen, fent over by this *ho-
norary* kind of *tranfportation*. And, by the
bye, I cannot help thinking, that our
Great Men ingrafted on that ftock, ought
to carry fome diftinguifhing mark of their
belonging to that country. Suppofe, therefore, that, in thefe cafes, a Silver Badge
of S. P. for *St. Patrick*, fhould be worn
on the left fhoulder; and when any perfons are provided for on the *home lift*, I
would have a golden badge for the Right
fhoulder, with S. G. upon it, for *St. George*,
with the additional honour to the Wearers,

that

their names and *titles,* written in capitals,
fhould be hung up in *St. George*'s chapel
above the lift of the Poor Knights of *Wind-*
for.—But to return;

Whilft I have been inadvertently
tempted to expatiate on the general nature of thefe largeffes, this very digref-
fion has fuggefted to me the ftrongeft
argument in behalf of this Great M——r.—
To fum up every reafon that can be urged
in one fhort queftion, let me only afk you,
whether it would not be a moft unnatural
reproach on the gratitude of the nation, if
that perfon, who has generoufly beftowed
fo many great and honourable *Penfions,*
fhould remain in want of one himfelf? *Pe-*
timufque damufque viciffim, fays that honeft
verfe of *Horace,* founded in gratitude. This,
I think, fhould be the Motto of the whole
Band, and fhould be ftuck up in a confpi-

cuous

cuous part of the Beef-eater's room at court, to fhew every body, as they enter, what favours Statefmen may expect from each other : and the fame device might be properly ufed in another *certain place* for the information of young m———rs?——Upon the principles of this axiom, the expedient I would propofe to provide for this Great Man, is, that every L——d or C——r in this Kingdom, or the neighbouring one, poffeft of a Penfion, exceeding 1000 *l. per* year, fhould, by way of poundage, make him an allowance of 5 *l. per. cent.*——and then *he* too will perhaps be provided for, pretty near equal to his merits——more at leaft than any other perfon——as well as have both his fhoulders properly decorated, according to the abovementioned Propofal.

Ha-

Having thus endeavoured (as bound in gratitude) to carve out a handsome provision for this Great Man, as well as the other, it is high time to conclude. I cannot however take my final leave of you, without lamenting the general despondency which you tell me the *Secession* of the Right Honourable Annuitant occasions in the Country. Much of it appears also in town : but in my mind it argues a poor and mean spirit, unworthy of *Britons*, unworthy of men. Have we, for Heaven's Sake, but ONE honest and able man among us? I should be sorry to hear even our enemies say so. I will venture to say that there is at least ONE MORE, of whom I have a better opinion, than even of our Great Man. The Person I mean is no other than THE KING. He has al-

I   ready

ready manifefted the trueft affection for
his people : and why fhould we be alarm-
ed or difturbed at the cabals and intrigues
of our *fellow-fervants*, when we are af-
fured of the care and protection of our
MASTER ? He knows the juft limits by
which his Power is circumfcribed, and
defires not to enlarge its bounds. In like
manner let every officer of ftate honeftly
perform the duties of his place, and aim
at nothing more ! While they bawl in
oppofition, they complain that power is
dangerous in the hands of a Minifter;
but when they get into power themfelves,
they dare to complain of being manacled
and fettered. The Power of the *Britifh* Con-
ftitution is lodged in no ONE Man, or Set of
Men, but collectively in the Whole People.
It were to be wifhed, therefore, by all

HONEST

HONEST MEN, that this frightful *Chimæra* of a PRIME MINISTER—GREAT MAN— or whatever he may call himself—that has so long ftalked between the Throne and the people in this nation, were totally annihilated: and as is generally faid, that, at the late Coronation, his prefent Majefty found himfelf obliged to be *his own* BISHOP, *his own* HERALD, &c. happy would it be for *Great Britain*, if it fhould prove an Omen that in this aufpicious reign, He will be found alfo to prove HIS OWN MINISTER.

I am, my Dear Sir,

Your, &c.

POST-

POSTSCRIPT.

October 22, 1761.

I Cannot forbear the triumph of adding a Postscript to transmit immediately to you the following Paragraph from the *St. James*'s Chronicle of this Evening.

At a Court of Common Council held this Day at Guildhall, a Motion was made, that an Address should be presented to the Right Hon. William Pitt, Esq; for his past Services. After several Speeches against the Motion, by a learned Deputy, the Ques-

4

tion

tion was put, and upon holding up of Hands, there appeared

For addreſſing Mr. Pitt – – 109

Againſt it – – – – – – 15

Whereupon a Committee was appointed to draw up the ſaid Addreſs; and alſo, at the ſame Time, to requeſt of Mr. Pitt, that he would continue to purſue the ſame Patriotick Principles upon which he has hitherto acted.

This, I hope, will thoroughly convince you Country-gentlemen of your error. Our honeſt Citizens, you ſee, know his merits: and though his name, as an *Annuitant*, has been publiſhed and printed, like the Bankrupts, in the *London Gazette*, yet the ſagacious Com-

mon

FRENCH & INDIAN WAR.

/PITT (William)/ The Right Honourable Annuitant vindicated.
With a word or two in favour of the other Great Man, in case
of his resignation. In a Letter to a Friend in the Country.
London, J. Morgan, 1761. Pp. 66, lacking the half-title,
paper wrappers, 8vo
        Not in Sabin, scarce. Authorship undiscovered by Hal-
kett and Laing. Written in vindication of Pitt who had recently
resigned his position as Secretary of State, and retired on an
annuity, which the author contends was not a bride but a well-
earned reqard for his services during the perioe of the way
with France and the capture of Quebec, Louisbourg, Guadaloupe,
etc. The other Great Man was Sir Thomas Pelham Holles, Duke of
Newcastle, who had in 1757 formed a Coalition with Pitt, but
who, in 1762, having acquiesced in forcing Pitt out of office,
found he had but played into the hands of Lord Bute, and was also

forced to resign.